Rock
Patrol

backpack Mysteries

9705

a backpack Mystery

Rock Patrol

Mary carpenter reid

BETHANY HOUSE PUBLISHERS
MINNEAPOLIS, MINNESOTA 55438

Rock Patrol
Copyright © 1997
Mary Carpenter Reid

Cover and text illustrations by Paul Turnbaugh

Published by Bethany House Publishers
A Ministry of Bethany Fellowship, Inc.
11300 Hampshire Avenue South
Minneapolis, Minnesota 55438

Printed in the United States of America.

Library of Congress Cataloging-in-Publication Data

Reid, Mary.
    Rock patrol / by Mary Carpenter Reid.
       p. cm. — (A backpack mystery ; 6)
    Summary: Sisters Steff and Paulie try to stop the vandalism at the apartment complex where their shy cousin is employed as the building manager.
    ISBN 1–55661–720–8 (pbk.)
    [1. Vandalism—Fiction. 2. Apartment Houses—Fiction. 3. Sisters—Fiction. 4. Christian life—Fiction. 5. Mystery and detective stories.] I. Title. II. Series: Reid, Mary. Backpack mystery ; 6.
PZ7.R2727Ro   1997
[Fic]—dc21   97–21039
                                               CIP
                                               AC

To a fellow in my family
named Jack.

MARY CARPENTER REID loves to visit places just like the places Steff and Paulie visit. Does she stay with peculiar relatives? That's her secret!

She will tell you her family is wonderful. She likes reading and writing children's books. She likes colors and computers. She especially likes getting letters from her readers.

She can't organize things as well as Steff does, but she makes lots of lists.

Two cats—a calico and a tiger cat—live at her house in California. *They* are very peculiar!

CONTENTS

. . . The Lord looks at the heart.

1 Samuel 16:7

tHirty-eigHt LigHt buLbs

"Uh-oh, I forgot something important." Steff Larson stopped on her way up the stairs in Cousin Emily Jane's apartment. She put down a suitcase and called over the railing to Emily Jane, "Really important."

Behind Steff came her younger sister, Paulie. Paulie held a basketball in one arm.

She tried to squeeze by Steff and the suitcase. Her backpack knocked against the wall. She wobbled, spun around, and dropped the basketball.

It rolled down the stairs and hit the tile floor by the front door with a loud *BOUNCE— BOUNCE—BOUNCE!*

Steff shuddered. Their father had left them here with Emily Jane only ten minutes before. He had warned them that his cousin was quiet and shy. Already Paulie was making unnecessary noise.

Emily Jane didn't seem upset. She tossed the basketball back to Paulie. "What did you forget, Steff?" she asked.

"To tell you that the entrance to your apartment complex is pretty dark. We almost drove right by."

"Yes," said Paulie. "We could hardly see the Princess Gardens sign."

"Oh no! Don't tell me someone has broken all thirty-eight light bulbs!" Now Emily Jane did seem upset.

She clapped her hands over her brown curls and moaned. "Ninety-five percent of the time, Princess Gardens is a lovely place. But lately, we've had a problem with vandalism."

Paulie whispered to Steff, "How does she know there are thirty-eight light bulbs?"

"Dad said she remembers things like that."

Emily Jane muttered, as if scolding herself, "I'm the apartment manager. I should be able to stop the problem. Why do I feel so helpless? Perhaps if I were older or more bold or . . ."

She put on a violet-colored jacket. They went outside.

"Last week, someone toilet-papered the gate," Emily Jane said. "Another time, I found our sign plastered with mud. Our maintenance man works and works, cleaning up the damage caused by the vandals."

The entrance was dark except for light that came from outside the complex.

"There should be lights everywhere— shining in the trees and in the bushes." Emily Jane pointed to a row of tiny flagpoles on top of the Princess Gardens sign. "You can't even see the colors in our little flags. Most of them are violet."

Steff tried to be cheerful. "It's not your fault

people go around tearing up things."

"I wonder what your father thought. I'm surprised he even left you with me."

"He had to," said Paulie. "He and Mom are going on their business trip."

"Oh, Paulie! He wouldn't leave us if he was worried," Steff told her.

"Well," said Emily Jane, "this is another job for Mr. Fix-It. That's what everyone calls our maintenance man. He'll fix the lights tomorrow."

Steff felt a hard lump under her shoe. She picked up a metal button. "Look what I found."

Paulie held out her hand. "I want that if you don't."

Steff gave it to her.

They started back to Emily Jane's apartment.

"The police think the vandals are people who live here in the complex," said Emily Jane. "Our own tenants."

"Vandals . . . here?" Paulie's voice squeaked.

"How many tenants do you have?" asked Steff.

Emily Jane said, "There are four units in each of our thirty buildings. That's 120 apartments."

"That's a lot of people," said Steff.

"And a lot of numbers," murmured Paulie.

Steff said, "Princess Gardens seems like a nice place to live. Why would any tenant want to spoil it?"

Emily Jane sighed. "Maybe I'm not a good manager."

Steff sighed, too. Sometimes, coming to stay in a new place was not easy—especially if your father's cousin was the most timid person in the world and your neighbors were vandals.

2

Yellow Hair

The next morning, Emily Jane showed the girls her office. "See, I can walk right in from my living room." She pointed to another door. It led outside to the front yard. "Other people use that door when they come to the office."

On the wooden desk was a sign that read *Manager.* Next to the sign was a violet plant.

Emily Jane pinched off a dry leaf. "The company I work for manages this apartment complex and many others. I want to have a career in apartment management." She looked worried. "I just don't know if I can."

"Mom thinks you're shy," said Paulie. "She wishes you had more self-confidence."

Steff sent her sister a warning look.

Paulie saw it and clamped her lips together.

Emily Jane agreed. "I guess I am shy."

The office telephone rang. Emily Jane told the caller, "Twenty-seven percent of leaky pipes under kitchen sinks can cause major repair jobs. I'll get Mr. Fix-It over there right away."

The caller kept talking.

Emily Jane frowned. "Yes, Mr. Nate, the U-shaped trap. Are you *sure* you know how to replace a rusty pipe yourself?" She listened, still frowning. "All right. I'll leave a new one by your door."

She hung up. "Mr. Nate is the tenant in apartment number 84. He never wants anyone to go in his apartment—even to repair things."

Steff looked out the office window. A boy about her age and a girl a little smaller than Paulie ran across the lawn. Their denim jackets flapped open. Book bags bounced on their backs.

The boy's yellow hair stuck up in spikes. He caught a skinny tree, swung around it, and kept running.

The girl chased him. She had frizzy yellow hair. It flopped over her shoulders like a curly mop.

"She needs barrettes," said Steff.

Suddenly, the boy scooped up a rock and threw it toward the girl.

She yelled at him, "Great throw, Butch! You missed me by a mile."

They both laughed.

But the rock smacked against the building near the office window.

Steff jerked open the door and ran outside. Paulie followed.

"Hey! You almost broke our window!" shouted Steff.

Both children stopped and stared at Steff. The girl pulled her hair back to see better.

Butch retorted, "We didn't break anything."

"Naah!" said the girl.

"Don't you know not to throw rocks?" shrieked Steff. "You want to kill somebody?"

Butch grinned. "Hey, Betts! Did I kill you? Tell this buttinsky you're not dead."

Steff gasped. She was not used to being called a buttinsky.

Betts giggled. "My brother didn't kill me."

"Who are you, anyway?" Butch sneered at Steff. "Is this some kind of Rock Patrol? And who's that little Rock Ranger behind you?"

"What did you call her?" demanded Steff.

Paulie said firmly, "My name is Paulie Larson. This is my sister, Steff. Our cousin is the manager of all these apartments."

Emily Jane came out. "Children," she said timidly, "I don't think throwing rocks is a good idea."

Steff waited for her to say more. When she didn't, Steff warned, "My cousin had better not catch you doing that again!"

The boy yelled, "Oops! The bus is coming!"

Betts and Butch ran out of the complex to the main street. A yellow school bus stopped at the corner. They climbed in.

Paulie asked, "Was he really trying to hit his sister with that rock?"

"Who knows?" answered Steff.

"Thirty-nine percent of children hit by flying objects need stitches," said Emily Jane.

Steff stepped back into the apartment.

Something swished across the floor. It tangled with her feet. She lost her balance and began to fall.

3

queeN of the
stairway

Steff landed on her stomach. "O-o-w-w!"

Paulie scolded, "Steff, you almost squashed a cat!"

"Cat? What about me? I'm the one that's squashed."

Paulie yelled out the door, "Emily Jane, a cat ran upstairs in your apartment. Steff almost squashed it."

Emily Jane rushed in. "Steff, are you hurt?"

Steff rubbed one elbow. "I guess not."

"I forgot to tell you about my cat," said Emily Jane.

"You have a cat?" Paulie cried. "Oh, good! We can play with it."

Emily Jane looked doubtful. "Victoria is very shy. She never gets close to anyone except me."

"Not anyone?" Paulie asked sadly.

"Not even my husband. Of course, he is away this week. But when he's home, she hides from him, too."

"What color is she?"

"Black and white and gray, with a touch of tan. Her fur is long and fluffy. Sometimes she sits on the stairs. I call her Queen of the Stairway."

"Where does she sleep?" asked Steff.

"I don't know. Someplace in the apartment. She never goes outside."

Emily Jane showed them that the door leading from the kitchen to the garage was propped open a few inches. "Her food and water are in the garage."

"A violet-colored litter box!" exclaimed Paulie. "How cute."

The office doorbell rang. A delivery man complained to Emily Jane. "The tenant in apartment number 17 bought a new television from our store. I'm supposed to deliver it, but no one answers the door. I can't hang around all day. How about letting me in to hook it up?"

Emily Jane said, "I'm sorry. Not without asking the tenant."

"Lady, you're the manager! Did you lose your keys or something?"

"No, but—"

"Well, then, let me in that apartment!"

Steff and Paulie watched from the living room.

Paulie made a grim face and jabbed one thumb toward the floor.

Emily Jane told the man, "The tenant may be at work. I'll try calling her there."

She made several calls. Finally, she said, "I'm sorry. I can't locate the tenant."

He spit on the sidewalk and stomped toward his truck.

Steff and Paulie marched into the office.

"How rude!" exclaimed Steff. "That man should have thanked you for trying to help."

Emily Jane made a funny noise in her throat. "Look at me—almost crying. I've been working here a year. I still get upset over impolite people. How can I expect to handle important matters like . . ."

"Like what?" asked Steff.

"Vandalism." Emily Jane dabbed at her eyes. "If I don't stop the vandalism soon, I won't get the promotion I want."

"Promotion to what?"

"To a new job in the main office of the management company. It begins two months from now."

"You'll get the new job," said Paulie.

Emily Jane shook her head. "People may think I'm not a strong enough person to handle it."

Steff told her, "Paulie and I will be on the lookout for the vandals, won't we?"

Paulie answered, "Sure."

Steff didn't think they would have to look far. Butch and Betts were definitely the vandal type. She'd keep an eye on them and catch them doing something wrong.

teddy bear man

A few minutes later, Steff and Paulie saw a strange sight out the office window.

A man pulling a child's red wagon rang the doorbell.

Paulie said, "That man looks like a teddy bear."

Steff agreed. He was plump. His bushy beard was the color of cinnamon, with a few gray streaks. So was the hair that showed under his blue baseball cap. Two brown button eyes dotted his wrinkled face.

Emily Jane opened the door. "Hi there, Mr. Fix-It!" She gave him an envelope. "Here are the work orders for today."

She introduced the girls. "Steff and Paulie are staying with me this week."

"Well, now," said the teddy bear man, "I've been at Princess Gardens a long time. We've never had two prettier princesses come to visit us."

The girls giggled. Of course, Steff knew he was just saying that.

Paulie asked about the red wagon.

"I use it to carry my toolbox and whatever else I need."

"We have a gardener," said Emily Jane. "But Mr. Fix-It does ninety percent of our other work. Speaking of work, Mr. Fix-It, I'm afraid the vandals hit again last night."

"Those rascals!" he exclaimed.

"All thirty-eight bulbs at the entrance need replacing."

"Don't worry, I'll fix the lights. Of course," he rubbed his cinnamon-colored beard, "I may need to work overtime to do it."

"Write the extra hours on your time sheet," said Emily Jane. "You'll be paid for them."

The telephone rang, and she went to her desk.

Mr. Fix-It winked at the girls. "Here's a riddle for you.

I have legs, but do not walk.
I have arms, but do not carry.
I have a seat, but do not sit.
What am I?"

They looked at each other and shrugged.

Mr. Fix-It's brown button eyes sparkled. "A chair."

He turned his wagon around and left.

"I wonder if he's somebody's grandfather," said Paulie.

"Nope," Steff grinned. "He's somebody's teddy bear."

Emily Jane was saying on the telephone, "Yes, five o'clock will be fine. A change? What kind of change?"

Emily Jane's hands shook as she hung up the phone. "Ms. Cruz is my boss. She's coming here at five o'clock to talk about my promotion. She wouldn't say more."

"What has she got to do with your promotion?" asked Steff.

Emily Jane gave a nervous laugh. "A lot. The management company will ask her how well I am doing my job here. If I stop the vandalism, she will say I should be promoted. If I don't, she won't."

Steff and Paulie brought their schoolwork to the living room. Steff could see into the office. She paid more attention to Emily Jane's work than she did to her own.

People called wanting to rent apartments. Tenants called about stopped-up toilets or broken dishwashers.

"I try to get every water problem fixed right away," Emily Jane told the girls. "Water damage can lead to big repair bills."

Twice she took her keys and clipboard and went to show people an apartment for rent.

She ordered new filters for Mr. Fix-It to put in every furnace. She explained, "Our furnaces last seventeen percent longer when filters are replaced often."

Steff said thoughtfully, "You must save lots of money by taking good care of the apartments. I could look through the old records in your office and see . . ." Steff slammed her math book shut. "I've got it! I'll do a report about the costs of repairs *before* you became manager and the costs *after* you became manager. I'll call the report *Repair Costs—Before and After*."

Paulie said, "That sounds good. When the management company sees all the money you're saving, you'll get promoted."

Emily Jane swung her office chair around and went back to work, saying, "*If* I stop the vandalism."

Steff called, "We're working on that, too."

"We are?" whispered Paulie. "How?"

"I've decided we should inspect the entire complex every four hours," Steff told her. "We'll make a schedule."

"Let me make it," begged Paulie.

"OK. I'll show you how."

"No, you make the squares too tiny."

"I do not." Steff got a ruler from her backpack. "Of course, we can't expect any vandalism until after Butch and Betts get home from school."

At five o'clock, Emily Jane's boss came. Ms. Cruz was big, and she had a big voice. She squeezed herself into a visitor's chair at Emily Jane's desk.

Steff and Paulie stayed in the living room.

Emily Jane asked, "What is this change that concerns my promotion?"

Ms. Cruz tucked a loose strand of dark hair behind her ear. "The management company is going to fill that job you want early. Next week."

"So soon?"

"Yes, and unless the vandalism at Princess Gardens stops, I'm afraid your chances of being promoted are not good."

Ms. Cruz tapped a polished fingernail on the arm of the chair. "Remember, one week from today the company will decide who gets the job."

5

Vandalism for Sure!

Steff whispered to Paulie, "Next week! Let's go check on those weird kids. I know their building."

They waved at Emily Jane and tiptoed from the living room.

It was almost dark. Few people were around.

The building where Butch and Betts lived had four apartments—just like all the buildings. The front doors of the four apartments were on one side. The four garages were attached to the back. A driveway came from the street and ran past the four garage doors. The driveway ended at a grassy area.

Steff and Paulie walked along the sidewalk. "Act as if we're just passing by," said Steff.

They heard noises by the garages and peeked around the corner of the building.

"Aha!" hissed Steff. "Look!"

Each building had an open compartment by the garages. Inside it was a huge trash container where all four families put their trash. Nearby were baskets of newspapers, cans, and glass waiting to be recycled.

The large trash container had been rolled out of its compartment. Betts was standing on Butch's knee, reaching inside the container.

"Caught them!" whispered Steff. "They're taking out trash to throw around. It's a good thing we came."

Betts waved something in the air and jumped down.

Paulie said, "She's got a bunch of dry weeds."

Butch gave the trash container a shove. It

rolled into the baskets. The baskets toppled. Newspapers slid across the driveway. Cans and bottles spilled.

"That's vandalism for sure!" Steff told Paulie.

They ran toward the kids.

Steff yelled, "You'd better stop that!"

Butch snarled, "Who says so? Oh, look, it's the Rock Patrol!"

"You're in trouble!" warned Steff.

Betts edged behind Butch. "Don't yell at my brother."

Paulie crowded close to Steff. "Don't yell at my sister."

Steff put her hands on her hips, leaned forward, and squinted her eyes. "You two are going to clean up that mess, or I'm calling the police."

She heard Paulie gasp, but she didn't care. She ordered, "Pick it up, or I'm calling the police."

Butch took a step toward her. "Oh, yeah!" he growled. "Well, my father is a policeman. What do you think of that?"

"Right! Sure he is!" Steff took a step toward him.

"Well, he is!" Butch took another step and made an ugly face.

They stood so close Steff saw threads hanging from Butch's denim jacket where a button was missing.

She tried to decide what to do next if they wouldn't clean up the mess.

Betts suddenly yelled, "Butch, we have to go in now."

She was looking at a window above the garage. Steff looked, too. A light clicked off and on.

Quickly, Butch rolled the trash container back in place. He and Betts tossed the papers, cans, and bottles into the baskets. Then they ran. Betts took the bunch of dry weeds with her.

Steff tried not to show how glad she was to see them go.

Paulie said, "It was good that Betts saw that light, huh?"

Steff ignored her. "What a joke! Their father is a policeman! Who would believe that?"

On the way back to Emily Jane's, the girls saw a tall man stepping out of apartment number 84. He wore jeans and a denim jacket. He walked toward them.

"That must be the man who doesn't want people in his apartment," said Steff.

Mr. Nate kept his head down. He seemed to be scowling. He took up most of the sidewalk as they met.

Steff thought maybe he couldn't see well. His glasses were thick.

6

aNother job for Mr. fix-it

At the apartment, Emily Jane sat in a corner of the living-room sofa. A dark gray fur ball bounded from the coffee table and vanished up the stairs.

"Victoria!" called Paulie.

"I'm sorry she isn't more friendly," said Emily Jane.

"Does she purr?"

"Never. She doesn't even meow. Once in a while, she makes a squeaky little *meee*."

"Where did you get her?"

"I found her in a parking lot when she was very young. She was frightened. Maybe she's still a little frightened."

The girls told their cousin about Butch and Betts and the trash.

"They probably didn't mean any harm," said Emily Jane.

Steff doubted that.

Emily Jane said, "I know it's not easy to like those two children. But I try to remember what the Bible says in 1 Samuel 16:7, '. . . The Lord looks at the heart.'"

Paulie asked, "Do you remember Bible verses like you remember percents of things?"

Emily Jane laughed. "Only some."

Steff said, "When I see Butch and Betts behaving badly, I don't like it." Then she chuckled. "Actually, I don't think I like the way Butch's yellow hair sticks up in spikes."

Emily Jane said gently, "You don't have to like how people act or how people look. But the Bible says we can't judge whether people are good or bad. Only God knows what is in their hearts."

In bed later, Paulie said, "I got to talk to Mom a long time tonight. She and Dad miss us. She asked if Emily Jane was still shy. I said yes."

"Dad and I talked about people's hearts." Steff stared at the dark ceiling. "He said he has been fooled by people who seemed one way on the outside. But on the inside, they were different."

Sometime later, Steff thought she heard a sound—a faint rustling sound. It seemed very close.

She hung down over the edge of the bed. Her hair touched the floor. She clicked on her flashlight and swept the circle of light back and forth underneath the box springs. She saw nothing.

The wind began to blow. It blew harder and harder.

The next morning, the wind still blew. Emily Jane and the girls found a surprise outside the office window.

"It's a blizzard," said Steff. "A blizzard of newspapers."

Hundreds of newspaper pages blew across the grass, swirled in clouds over the street, caught in the bushes, and piled up between buildings.

"This has never happened before," said Emily Jane.

Steff said, "Another job for Mr. Fix-It."

She was thinking about Betts and Butch knocking over the recycle baskets. She remembered the newspapers spilling on the driveway. Every building had a recycle basket for newspapers.

Then Steff remembered something else. She pulled Paulie aside. "Where's the metal button I found at the entrance the night we came?"

Paulie had it in her backpack.

Steff looked at it. "There was a button missing from Butch's denim jacket last night. I think this is the button. It might have come off when those kids were breaking the lights."

"Oooh," said Paulie.

"Yes, Butch and Betts are looking more and more like vandals."

Mr. Fix-It came to clean up. The wind kept blowing the pages out of his reach.

Steff thought he must be tired. She asked Emily Jane, "May Paulie and I help Mr. Fix-It collect the papers?"

Emily Jane said, "That would be nice."

Outside, Paulie laughed each time the wind snatched a page from Steff's fingertips.

"Don't laugh at me," said Steff. "You're not catching any, either."

"I'll jump on them, and you come get them," said Paulie.

Mr. Fix-It stacked what they gathered in his wagon and put a rock on top.

Finally, the wind stopped.

Steff peeled off pages that had snagged on the fence around the pool. She felt a little thump on the back of her head. Then another. She turned in time to duck a ball of paper flying through the air like a snowball. "Stop that, Paulie!"

Paulie giggled. "It's not me!"

Then Steff saw that Mr. Fix-It had made paper balls. He was laughing and throwing them at the girls.

Steff made one and ran close enough to hit Mr. Fix-It. She yelled, "Let's get him, Paulie!"

"No fair, girls. Two against one! Remember, I'm an old man."

A woman from a nearby apartment brought a cup of coffee to Mr. Fix-It. "I know how you like cream. Did I put in enough?"

He took a sip. "Ahh . . . perfect."

While he drank his coffee, the girls finished picking up papers on the basketball court.

Before Mr. Fix-It left, he said, "Got another riddle for you.

What's lighter than a feather, but you can't hold it for even five minutes?"

"That could be a lot of things," said Steff. But she couldn't think of any.

"What is it?" asked Paulie.

Mr. Fix-It grinned. "Your breath."

On the way back to Emily Jane's apartment, Paulie said, "Everybody sure likes the teddy bear man."

7

i dare you!

Later that morning, Emily Jane talked to the gardener about putting fertilizer on the grass.

Then she and the girls walked through the complex.

One building had no window screens on the first floor. They found them stuffed in a trash container.

"These are ruined. I'll have to order new screens." Emily Jane wrote on her clipboard. "Another job for Mr. Fix-It."

"Vandalism is dumb," said Steff.

On the next street, Emily Jane waved to a police officer driving past.

Paulie said, "He's looking for vandals, isn't he?"

"Actually, that man lives here. He's the father of Betts and Butch."

"You're kidding!" exclaimed Steff. "Their father really is a policeman!"

"Look, his hair is yellow, too," said Paulie.

Steff asked, "What happens when a policeman's kids get arrested?"

Emily Jane looked shocked. "Whatever made you think of that?"

"I just wondered."

That afternoon, Steff and Paulie watched for Butch and Betts to get off the school bus. The girls followed them and then hung around the front of their building.

"Are they going to stay in there all night?" complained Paulie. "We can't catch them being vandals if they don't come out and wreck something."

The front door opened.

"Finally! Here comes Betts," said Steff.

"She's carrying a rug," said Paulie. "Now she's waving it."

Snap! Betts shook the rug. *Snap!*

"Must be a signal," said Steff. She looked around for a possible co-vandal.

Betts had left the front door open. Butch was in the living room. A motor whined.

"That's a vacuum cleaner," said Paulie. "Butch is running a vacuum. They're not sending signals. They're cleaning house!"

Steff felt silly. But she said, "We still have to keep an eye on them."

Betts went inside and shut the door.

Paulie groaned. "I'm hungry. Can we go?"

As they turned away, Butch came out of the apartment.

He shouted, "Hey, it's the Rock Patrol! Still want to call the police? Call my dad!" He held a fist to his ear and chanted, "Rock Patrol calling! Rock Patrol calling!"

"Pretend we didn't hear," Steff told Paulie.

"I dare you to call my dad!" yelled Butch.

Betts shouted from inside the apartment, "Butch, come here!"

Steff couldn't stand it. She hollered at Butch, "OK! So your dad is a policeman. So what?"

"Butch!" Betts shouted again. "Come help me open this can of soup."

"OK, OK!" Butch headed for the front door.

Steff told her sister, "You know what? I really don't like that guy's spiky yellow hair. I don't like her hair, either."

As they left, Steff glanced at a back window upstairs in Butch's apartment. The curtains were open. She saw something odd. All the buildings were like Emily Jane's, so Steff knew that room was the biggest bedroom. It would not belong to Betts.

She asked Paulie, "Remember the weeds Betts took from the trash? There they are—in a vase on the windowsill."

"Hmm," said Paulie. "In a vase, they almost look like dried-up flowers."

"Maybe. But why would anybody keep scraggly, old dried-up anything?"

a ſquare world

The next day, Steff and Paulie followed their schedule. Every four hours, they walked around the complex. Sometimes Emily Jane went with them. Sometimes Steff and Paulie took their ball and stopped to shoot baskets.

After dinner that night, Paulie said, "I'm going to find where Victoria sleeps. I'll start in the garage."

Emily Jane warned, "Seventy-seven percent of Victoria's hiding places are at least five feet above the floor."

Steff frowned. Was she teasing? "Seventy-seven percent? Are you sure?"

Emily Jane winked. "Could be."

Steff thought that sometimes—maybe four percent of the time—her cousin was kidding about percents.

Emily Jane said, "I'll be back soon. I have to drop off this new pipe at Mr. Nate's front door. Oh, I wish he would let Mr. Fix-It do the job."

Steff sat at Emily Jane's desk and worked on *Repair Costs—Before and After.*

Paulie came into the office carrying three long ribbons—violet, silver, and pink. She said, "I can't find that cat anywhere."

"What are you doing with those ribbons?" asked Steff.

"I'm braiding a crown for Victoria."

Just then, Steff saw something out the office window. "Vandalism!" she exclaimed. "It's happening right now!"

"What? Where?" Paulie darted to the window.

"Come on! If we hurry, we can stop it."

They ran outside.

A girl with frizzy yellow hair raced down the sidewalk. She carried a square cardboard box in one hand. In the other were three tiny flagpoles with little plastic flags. It was Betts.

Steff leaped in front of her and held her arms wide. "Stop! Did you take those flags off the Princess Gardens sign?"

Betts tried to dodge around Steff. "I was coming to the office to ask if I could borrow them."

"Oh?" Steff raised her eyebrows as high as they would go.

"Why do you want them?" asked Paulie.

"For my school project. This box is going to be the world. I need flagpoles with flags to put on top."

Paulie looked amazed. "That's a square box. You're making a square world?"

Betts broke into tears. She pushed her hair back and wiped her eyes. "I don't have a round box."

Steff was pretty sure Betts had not been headed for the office. But to make the world out of a square box? No way!

"Come in the office," Steff muttered. "Call your father. Ask if you can stay and work on your project."

"He doesn't come home until nine o'clock. I can call my brother."

Steff wondered if Butch would answer the phone. He could be out somewhere—getting into mischief.

But Butch did answer and said okay.

Emily Jane returned. She let Betts borrow the flags.

Steff asked Betts, "Do you have to make the whole earth?"

"I guess not."

"Good, I have an idea. Paulie, bring washable markers from your backpack. Emily Jane, could you please help cut this box?"

An hour later, Emily Jane walked Betts home.

Betts carried her project.

The sides of the box had been cut to four inches. Betts had turned it upside down and drawn a map of Canada, the United States, and

Mexico. She colored the Princess Gardens plastic flags to look like the flags of those three countries. She poked the flagpoles through the box so they stood up. The flags waved as she walked.

While the girls got ready for bed, Steff said, "I wonder if Betts really was going to ask to borrow the flags."

Paulie spit blue toothpaste. "Did you know their mother has been sick a long time? She mostly stays in her bedroom."

Steff remembered the dried-up weeds in the window. Betts must have given them to her mother.

"Betts told me," said Paulie, "that she and Butch do almost all the work, cleaning and cooking—everything."

Steff put away her hairbrush. "I'm glad we helped with her project, even if those kids are troublemakers."

The girls went down and said good-night to Emily Jane.

At the foot of the stairs, Steff told Paulie, "Beat you to bed!"

"No, you won't!"

They raced up to their room and leaped on the beds.

Steff bounced on her violet-covered bedspread much harder than she intended. The bed made terrible noises.

Paulie cried, "Oh, my goodness! You broke it!"

9

victoria's bed

The bed groaned and settled down. It didn't look broken.

Then came a shrill little *meee*. A shadow streaked from under Steff's bed, across the room, and out the door.

Both girls threw themselves on the floor and looked under the bed.

The bottom of the box springs was covered with thin cloth. In the middle of the cloth was a ragged hole about the size of a cat.

"Here's where Victoria sleeps!" Paulie

scooted on her back under the bed and tried to see up inside the box springs.

"That's why I've heard noises at night," said Steff.

"Cats like cozy places."

Steff laughed. "Sure! One in five billion cats sleeps inside cozy box springs."

The next day, the girls followed their schedule and watched Butch and Betts when they came home from school. But nothing happened.

After dinner, Victoria came out of hiding and posed like a statue near the top of the stairs.

Paulie was thrilled. She sat on the bottom step, trying to coax Victoria down to the living room.

"Kitty, kitty . . . come on, Queen of the Stairway. We won't hurt you. Come on, kitty."

Finally, Victoria slinked down one step. The jewels on her violet-colored collar twinkled as she moved.

Steff sat on the floor by the coffee table with copies of Mr. Fix-It's work orders.

Paulie scolded, "Don't rattle those papers.

You're scaring Victoria."

"I have to work on *Repair Costs—Before and After*. It's showing that Emily Jane is a great manager."

"Kitty, kitty . . . please come down, Victoria," cooed Paulie.

Victoria slinked down another step, then another.

"Look," Paulie said, still using her coaxing voice. "She's almost letting me touch her."

Emily Jane came down the stairs. She stopped above Victoria. "Why, Paulie, I think my cat is beginning to feel comfortable around you."

Paulie put her hand out ever so slowly . . . closer and closer . . . until . . . "I'm touching Victoria!" she whispered softly.

Steff got a good look at Victoria. She was a beautiful cat. Her long, dark fur shone with shades of black and gray and a touch of tan. The sparkling white on her stomach flowed up her chest and touched her sides here and there. Her paws were white, and a white triangle brightened her face.

Paulie kept cooing, gently stroking Victoria.

Suddenly, the doorbell rang. In the quiet house, it clanged like the Liberty Bell. Even Steff jumped.

In a flash, the cat leaped over Paulie, hit the floor, and disappeared.

"Oh no!" cried Paulie. "Just when she let me touch her."

Emily Jane said, "That must be my boss. We're making a night inspection of Princess Gardens—a lighting and safety check. Safety is the second biggest worry of eighty-two percent of apartment managers."

She opened the front door.

It was not Ms. Cruz.

Instead, a woman from the next building held up an envelope. "Some of your mail got in my mailbox."

Before Emily Jane could take it, the telephone rang.

"Oh," she said. "Please excu-u-u-s—"

A flurry of motion skittered across the floor. It was Victoria. She darted between Emily Jane's feet.

The woman with the envelope shrieked and hopped out of the way.

Victoria streaked through the open door.

"Victoria, come back!" called Emily Jane. "Oh, dear! Both the doorbell and the phone! It was too much for her."

The telephone kept ringing.

Steff rushed to the door. "I'll get Victoria."

Paulie ran after her. "Me too."

But Victoria was out of sight.

gross! gross! gross!

"There's no telling where that cat went," Steff told Paulie. "We have to find her. Victoria is not used to being outside, and it's dark."

They hurried through the complex.

Near the pool, they spotted Mr. Nate. He quickly turned a corner, as if he didn't want to be seen.

They checked around the basketball court. They climbed all over the playground equipment.

"Kitty, kitty, kitty! Victoria! Please come out," begged Paulie.

At the building where Butch and Betts lived, they spotted something white near the garages.

"Kitty, kitty!" Paulie ran to see if it was Victoria.

She came back holding her nose. "It was only a big, crumpled bag. Something smells awful."

The next building was at the edge of the complex. They walked from the sidewalk up the driveway toward the garages on the back of the building.

"Phew!" said Paulie. "The smell is worse here."

On one side of the driveway were the four garages. On the other side, a row of big bushes grew in front of the block wall that ran around the outside of the complex. The driveway ended at a grassy area.

The driveway didn't feel right. It didn't feel the way a driveway should when you walk on it.

Something soft was scattered around in lumps and piles. At first, Steff thought it was black dirt. But dirt didn't smell like this.

They tiptoed past the four garage doors and hopped over on the clean grass.

A mound of empty white bags lay nearby. Steff read one. "*F-E-R-T-I-L-I-Z-E-R!*"

"Yuck!" said Paulie.

"It's cow manure!" cried Steff. "Double yuck!"

"Gross! Gross! Gross!" Paulie held her stomach. "We were walking on cow manure!"

"Somebody fertilized this driveway. How weird!"

"Yeah," Paulie snorted. "Like plants would grow on it!" She looked at the bag. "Know what? This is the same as the bag near Betts and Butch's building."

Steff shot a fist in the air and shouted, "Yes! We caught them! They put fertilizer on this driveway."

Paulie wiped her shoes on the grass. "The tenants won't like driving through fertilizer to get out of their garages. Emily Jane will have to ask Mr. Fix-It to clean it up tonight."

Steff suddenly remembered the night inspection. "Oh no! Emily Jane and Ms. Cruz might come at any minute. We can't wait for Mr. Fix-It. If Ms. Cruz sees this—"

"Or smells it!" cried Paulie.

"She'll never give Emily Jane that promotion. We have to clean it up ourselves— right now!"

They took the empty bags to the trash container.

A garden hose lay nearby. Steff turned on the water as hard as it would go.

"I'll try to wash the fertilizer into the grass where it won't show. Go find Emily Jane and Ms. Cruz. Keep them away as long as you can."

"OK, but you watch for Victoria."

Steff flooded the driveway. She moved the stream of water back and forth, pushing the fertilizer along.

She was furious at Betts and Butch. She wanted to leave the horrid gunk and let them get blamed. But they would say that one empty bag near their building didn't mean anything. She and Paulie would just have to keep watching those kids.

Dirty black water sloshed over Steff's tennis

shoes. She could almost feel slime oozing between her toes. Her jeans were wet to the knees.

She worked her way along the garages. Globs of wet fertilizer and pools of water collected at the end of the driveway. It was hard to wash everything into the grass.

She could see the next building now, the one where Butch and Betts lived.

Suddenly, a car came down the street. It turned into their driveway. She jumped back, hoping the driver hadn't seen her.

But a minute later, a man's voice boomed behind her. "What are you doing, young lady?"

Startled, Steff whirled around. Water shot from the hose and blasted the man's chest. Quickly, she swung the hose away from him. But the water hit a garage door and bounced back on both of them.

Frantic now, she jerked the hose this way and that. The powerful stream of cold water sprayed him again, this time in the face.

Steff was horrified. "I'm sorry—"

"Sorry?" the man sputtered. He grabbed the

hose. "You'll be sorry when your parents find out about this. I don't know who you are or where you live, but I can't understand why you made a filthy mess like this."

"Me?" Steff cried. "I didn't do anything wrong!"

big trouble

The man said, "Is that so? Maybe you can tell me what you know about *all* the vandalism at Princess Gardens."

The man wore a police officer's uniform—a sopping wet uniform—and he had yellow hair. It was Betts and Butch's father.

"You've got it wrong," Steff insisted. "I was cleaning the driveway."

Her heart sank. She was in big trouble! He would never believe that his own children were the vandals.

Water gushed from the hose in his hand. It arched high, like a basketball shot, and fell hard on the driveway.

Suddenly, someone else appeared.

Here was a person who could help. Steff dodged around the officer and ran to the man with the bushy beard. "Mr. Fix-It!"

"Huh?" His brown button eyes grew large. He looked at her, then at the officer, then at her again.

"Tell this policeman who I am," she begged.

Mr. Fix-It blubbered, "Er . . . uh . . . fertilizer! Somebody has made a dreadful mess."

"Please tell him I'm not a vandal. Tell him I'm just a visitor."

"Well, it's true that's she's visiting the manager." Mr. Fix-It turned to Steff. "This does look kind of bad for you, doesn't it?"

"What?" cried Steff.

Suddenly, Paulie dashed up from the sidewalk, pointing over her shoulder. Behind her came Emily Jane and Ms. Cruz.

Emily Jane gasped and dropped her clipboard.

Ms. Cruz boomed, "What's going on here?" She marched over and turned off the water. Then she glared at the policeman. "Who called the police?"

"No one." He waved the hose toward his building. The gush of water fizzled to a dribble. "I was—"

She didn't let him finish. She peered at Steff's wet clothes and demanded, "What do you know about this?"

Steff opened her mouth, but no words came out.

Emily Jane put her violet-colored jacket on Steff's shoulders. She picked up her clipboard and wiped it with a tissue. Then she spoke in the loudest, strongest voice Steff had ever heard her use.

"This police officer is a tenant in the next building. Steff and Paulie are looking for my lost cat. Mr. Fix-It is here. . . ." Her eyes opened wide. She slowly turned to Mr. Fix-It and asked, "Mr. Fix-It, what *are* you doing here?"

"I . . . I was taking a walk," he stammered.

Ms. Cruz roared, "None of that explains this disgusting driveway!"

Steff gulped and said as bravely as she could, "Paulie and I found fertilizer dumped here. I was trying to wash it off."

Ms. Cruz tapped one foot.

The officer twirled the end of the limp hose.

Mr. Fix-It suggested, "You might ask Mr. Nate in number 84 about this. He's an odd one. Keeps to himself. No telling what he's been up to."

The officer said, "Mr. Nate? That guy may be odd, but he's harmless. He works day and night in his apartment, writing computer programs. He told me he's afraid someone will come in to mess with his computers."

Suddenly, a dark fur ball raced out of the bushes by the block wall. It bounded across the driveway and jumped into Paulie's arms.

"Ooof!" Paulie fell back a step. "Victoria!" she cried. "You're letting me hold you."

Emily Jane exclaimed, "There's my cat!"

"Never mind the cat," said Ms. Cruz. "We have a problem."

"Phew! So does Victoria." Paulie wrinkled her nose and turned her head to one side. "She stinks."

"Why wouldn't she?" asked Ms. Cruz. "I'm sure we all smell like wet cow manure."

"Oh! My cat stays away from anything as nasty as that." Emily Jane felt Victoria's paws. "See, her feet are barely damp."

Paulie rubbed her fingers together. "Actually, Victoria's fur feels dusty."

"Hmm," murmured Steff. "I'll find out where she's been."

12

one Hundred percent

Mr. Fix-It said, "That's just a cat. Cats go everyplace."

"Victoria is not *just* a cat." Steff hurried toward the big bushes by the block wall.

She ducked behind them. It smelled bad here, too. She felt something hard under her feet. A wagon handle lay on the ground. Steff grabbed it and pulled. The wagon wouldn't budge. It must be loaded with something heavy. She backed up, tugging as hard as she could with both hands. The wagon moved. Slowly, Steff wheeled it out to the driveway.

It was Mr. Fix-It's wagon.

Steff saw what was on the wagon. So did everyone else.

She dropped the handle and stepped back.

Victoria squirmed in Paulie's arms. It was so quiet that even the tiny *meee* she made sounded loud.

"Oh." Mr. Fix-It took off his blue baseball cap and turned it around and around. "I wondered where I left my wagon." He put the cap back on. "I . . . I brought it when I came over here . . . er . . . to fix a broken faucet."

Steff began to get a sick feeling.

Emily Jane spoke firmly. "I wonder why there are no tools in your wagon, Mr. Fix-It. I wonder why it is stacked with bags of fertilizer."

"The gardener must have borrowed it."

"No," said Emily Jane. "He did not. The gardener put the fertilizer in the storage area. He planned to spread it on the grass next week."

"But . . . but," Steff stammered, "that means Mr. Fix-It put the fertilizer on this driveway!

Why would he do that?"

The police officer dropped the hose. He stepped over to Mr. Fix-It. "Yes, why?"

Mr. Fix-It pulled at his beard. "I was going to clean it up tomorrow. I always fix everything around here."

Steff moved close to her sister. "Oh, Paulie," she whispered. "I made a bad mistake. Butch and Betts are not vandals. Mr. Fix-It is."

Paulie said softly, "But he's the teddy bear man."

Emily Jane didn't seem shy now. She told Mr. Fix-It, "I think you felt like a hero for fixing all our problems, and you wanted to be paid for working more hours. So you've been making extra work for yourself."

"I had to." He glared at her. "Ever since you became manager, there has been less work for me to do. You always remember to take care of little problems, and they never grow into big repair jobs."

"From now on, there won't be *any* work for you here, Mr. Fix-It," snapped Ms. Cruz. "We do not let dishonest people work at Princess Gardens."

She turned to Emily Jane. "But we do promote people who deserve it. You'll get that new job."

Paulie poked Steff. "Hear that?"

Steff nodded. Emily Jane was being promoted, and no one had even looked at *Repair Costs—Before and After*.

Suddenly, a boy's voice yelled, "Dad! We heard your car."

Butch and Betts came along the driveway, jumping from one dry spot to another. Butch stopped.

Steff heard him mutter, "Not the Rock Patrol again!"

Betts said, "Daddy, we've been waiting for you. Mom is feeling better today. She helped us fix dinner, and—"

Butch shot out a hand to stop Betts. "What's wrong, Dad?"

"Everything is under control," said their father.

"But, Daddy, you're all wet," said Betts.

"Butch, take your sister home."

Betts made a face. "What stinks?"

"Go on, both of you. Tell your mother I'll be there soon."

Butch stuck out his lower lip as if he wasn't going anyplace. Finally, he grumbled, "Come on, Betts."

Steff felt awful. She had been so sure that Butch and Betts were the vandals. She hadn't liked the way they acted, and she hadn't liked the way they looked, so she had judged them. She had decided they were bad.

Oh, Lord, Steff prayed, *I'm so very sorry.*

She called after Butch and Betts, "See you guys tomorrow. We can shoot some baskets. OK?"

"Maybe," answered Butch.

Steff whispered to Paulie, "I suppose I could sew that button on his jacket."

Paulie said, "I'm going to ask Betts if she wants to make paper flowers to give to her mother. I can show her how."

Emily Jane hugged the girls and whispered,

"Good job, girls. You found the Princess Gardens vandal."

Paulie said, "Victoria helped."

Emily Jane rubbed Victoria behind the ears. "Take her home. I'll come in a minute."

On the way, Steff told Paulie, "I guess sometimes people like Mr. Fix-It can fool us. But I fooled myself about Betts and Butch. I only looked at them on the outside. I didn't even try to peek inside."

Paulie grinned. "We would have been surprised."

"There were lots of surprises tonight," said Steff. "Did you hear how boldly Emily Jane spoke to Mr. Fix-It and to Ms. Cruz? She's not as shy as we thought."

"And Mr. Fix-It is not as nice as we thought," said Paulie.

"And Betts and Butch are not as weird as we thought."

Emily Jane caught up. "Oh, Steff, I hope you can finish *Repair Costs—Before and After.* I want to show it to my new boss. The management company likes to hear about saving money."

Steff said, "It's almost finished. In fact, it is ninety-nine percent finished."

"Ninety-nine percent?" Paulie snickered. "Is anything *ever* one hundred percent of anything?"

"Of course," said Steff.

"Like what?"

Steff thought a moment. "The Bible says God looks at the heart. Yes, God looks at one hundred percent of hearts one hundred percent of the time."

Series for Young Readers*
From Bethany House Publishers

★ ★ ★

THE ADVENTURES OF CALLIE ANN
by Shannon Mason Leppard
Readers will giggle their way through the true-to-life escapades of Callie Ann Davies and her many North Carolina friends.

★ ★ ★

BACKPACK MYSTERIES
by Mary Carpenter Reid
This excitement-filled mystery series follows the mishaps and adventures of Steff and Paulie Larson as they strive to help often-eccentric relatives crack their toughest cases.

★ ★ ★

THE CUL-DE-SAC KIDS
by Beverly Lewis
Each story in this lighthearted series features the hilarious antics and predicaments of nine endearing boys and girls who live on Blossom Hill Lane.

★ ★ ★

RUBY SLIPPERS SCHOOL
by Stacy Towle Morgan
Join the fun as home-schoolers Hope and Annie Brown visit fascinating countries and meet inspiring Christians from around the world!

★ ★ ★

THREE COUSINS DETECTIVE CLUB®
by Elspeth Campbell Murphy
Famous detective cousins Timothy, Titus, and Sarah-Jane learn compelling Scripture-based truths while finding—and solving—intriguing mysteries.

* (ages 7–10)

9611